Opening Day
with Hattie & Calvin

follow your dreams

Written by
R. J. Kinderman

Illustrated by
Robert Andrea

SPINNING WHEELS PUBLISHING

© 2020 R. J. Kinderman

All rights reserved, including the right of reproduction in whole or in part in any form whatsoever.

Publisher's Cataloging-in-Publication Data
(provided by Five Rainbows Cataloging Services)

Names: Kinderman, R. J., author. | Andrea, Robert, illustrator.
Title: Opening day with Hattie & Calvin / written by R. J. Kinderman ; Robert Andrea, illustrator.
Description: Trego, WI : Spinning Wheels Publishing, 2020. | Series: Outdoors with Hattie & Calvin, bk. 1. | Summary: Two children learn about hunting, fishing, and firearms safety while gaining appreciation for the outdoors. | Audience: Grades K-2.
Identifiers: ISBN 978-0-9856469-9-8 (hardcover)
Subjects: LCSH: Picture books for children. | CYAC: Hunting--Fiction. | Fishing--Fiction. | Firearms--Safety measures--Fiction. | Boys--Fiction. | Girls--Fiction. | BISAC: JUVENILE FICTION / Sports & Recreation / Camping & Outdoor Activities. | JUVENILE FICTION / Social Themes / Self-Esteem & Self-Reliance. | JUVENILE FICTION / Readers / Beginner.

Editorial and design by Heather McElwain, Turtle Bay Creative

OTHER BOOKS BY
R. J. KINDERMAN and SPINNING WHEELS PUBLISHING:

To learn more, please visit
spinningwheelspublishing.com

Printed in the United States

To my father, Robert R. Kinderman, who started me on my hunting and fishing journey; my son, Ben; and my grandchildren, Hattie and Calvin—who inspired this book—as they dream about their first opening day.

—R. J. Kinderman

To my wonderful wife, Jill, and my family for their love, support, and encouragement. Thank you to the good Lord for my creatitive ability.

—Robert Andrea, John 3:16

Dad *loves* to hunt and fish.
He's big and he is strong.

He says when we are ready, we get to *come along*.

We *always* must be *careful* when handling a gun.

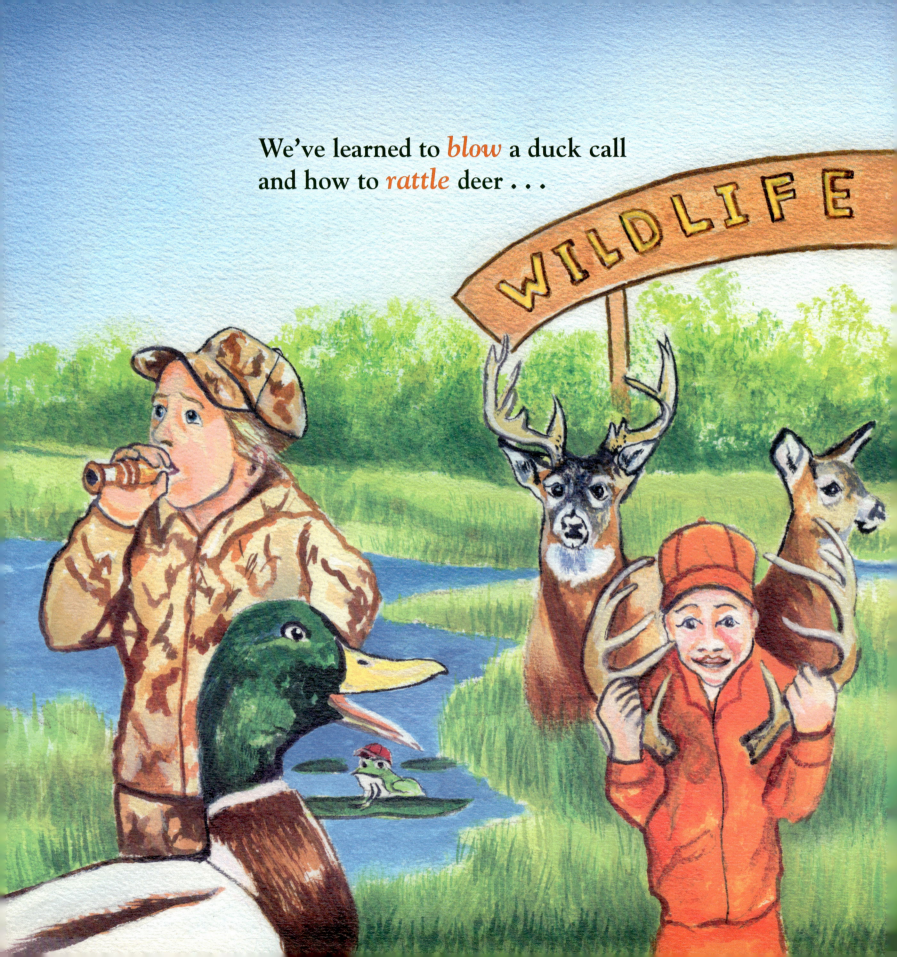

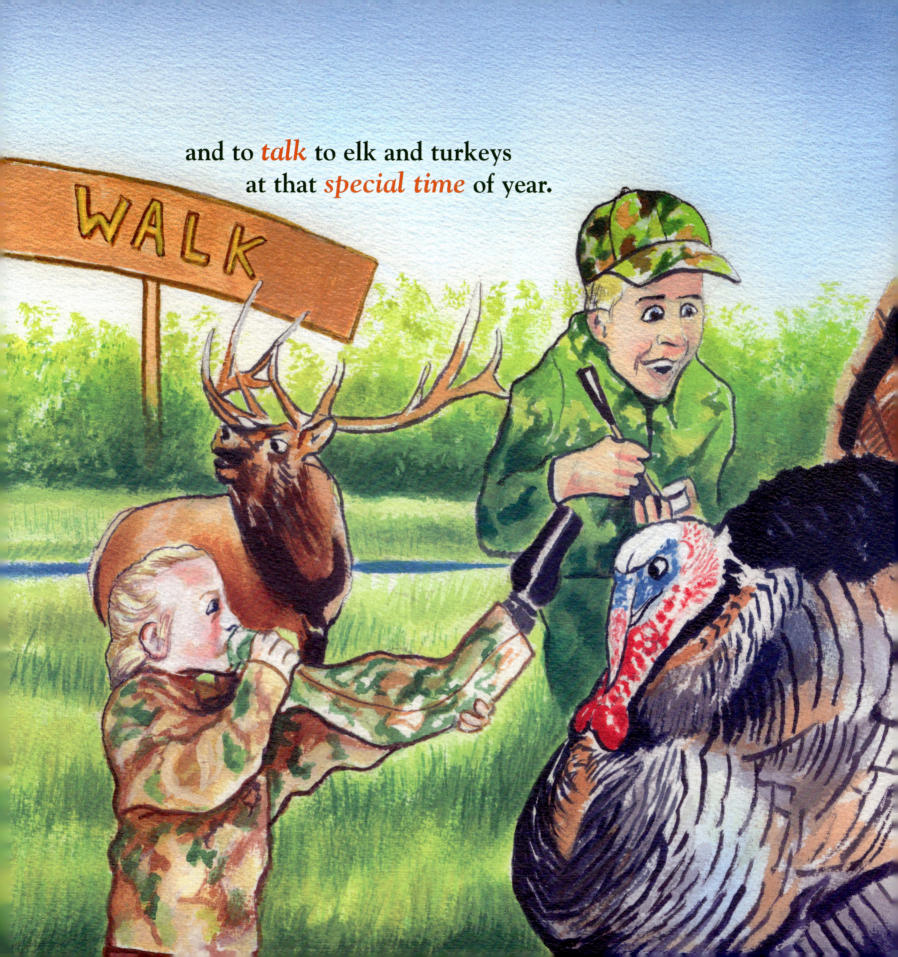

Dad wears *special* outdoor clothing.
He has guns and bows and gear.

Dad's *favorite* place for shopping makes him *smile ear to ear*.

We need *camo* for bow season, *blaze orange* to hunt with guns.

We *never* thought that shopping could *ever* be such fun.

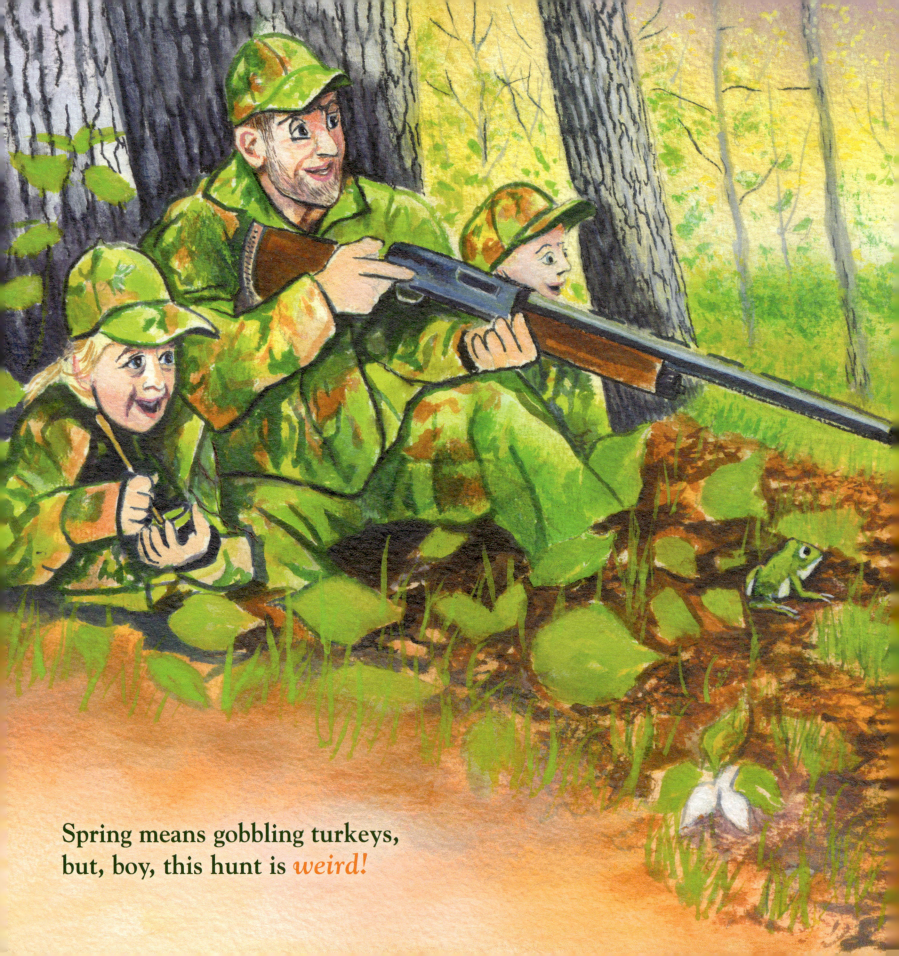

Spring means gobbling turkeys, but, boy, this hunt is *weird!*

We never thought we'd see a bird that has a 12-inch *beard!*

With tackle box, fishing poles,
life jackets, and live bait,
we're *on the water early,*
not wanting to be late.

Walleyes and perch are biting.
We have sandwiches and pop.
Grandpa catches a *whopper*.
We wish the fun would never stop.

As we pull up to the dock, Mom asks, "How was your day?" Dad tells mom the story of the *one that got away*.

Come fall, Ida flushes pheasants that *explode* out of our pockets . . .

They sail over cornfields—
like *colorful, cackling rockets.*

We *hide out* in our duck blind
in the crisp morning air,
and try to call in singles
or maybe even pairs.

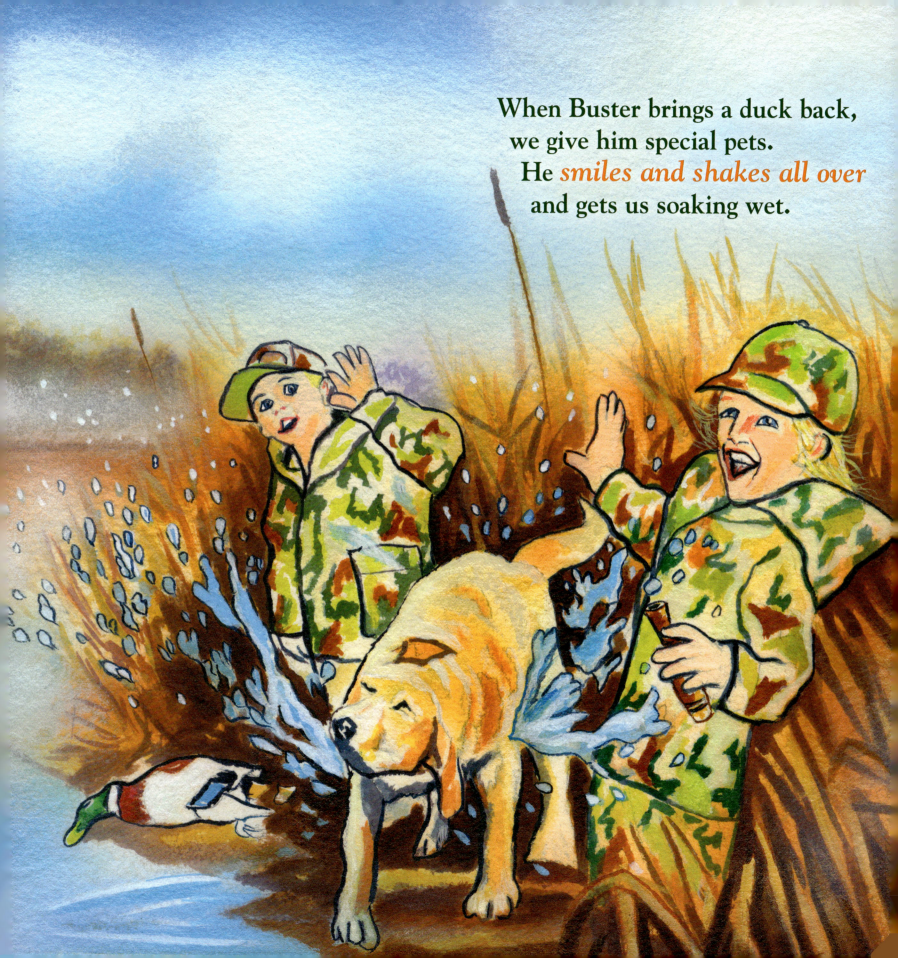

We ride high up in the mountains where big elk are *free to roam.*

Our wall tent nestled in the trees is our *home away from home.*

Sitting in our deer stand,
quietly eating lunch,
we hear a stick that *snaps*,
leaves that start to *crunch*.

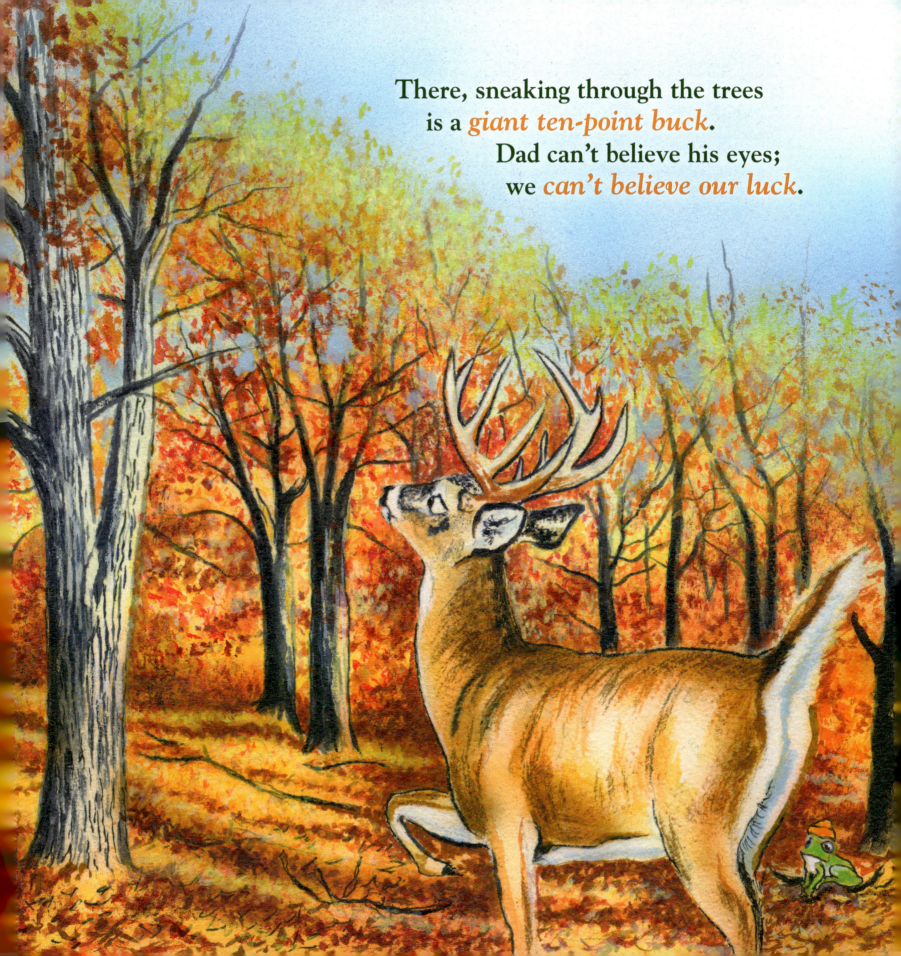

There, sneaking through the trees
is a *giant ten-point buck*.
Dad can't believe his eyes;
we *can't believe our luck*.

"WAKE UP! You both are ready. Today's *your special day!*"

We thought the dream was *our* dream,
but it was Dad's dream too.
He said, "Today's *my special day*
to be with both of you!"

OUR SPECIAL DAY